Follow My Leader

Tony Bradman

Illustrated by Priscilla Lamont

CAMBRIDGE
UNIVERSITY PRESS

It was playtime, but Neal and his friends
didn't know what to do.

Then Neal had a brilliant idea.

  "I know," he said. "Let's play Follow
My Leader!"

Paul was playing a quiet game.

But Neal and his friends soon stopped that.
Paul squealed.
"Follow My Leader!" laughed Neal.

Laura and a friend were playing
a hopping game.

But Neal and his friends soon stopped that.

The children squealed.

"Follow My Leader!" laughed Neal.

Kate and two friends were playing
a jumping game.

But Neal and his friends soon stopped that.
The children squealed.
"Follow My Leader!" laughed Neal.

Jodie and three friends were playing
a skipping game.

But Neal and his friends soon stopped that.

The children squealed.

"Follow My Leader!" laughed Neal.

"That was fun!" said Neal, and his friends laughed. But the others didn't.

They thought it was somebody else's
turn to squeal!

So, "Follow My Leader!" yelled Jodie.

Jodie and her friends chased the naughty
ones here, there and everywhere.

In the end, Miss Miller heard them squealing.
She laughed, and saved them – even Neal.

Next playtime, Neal's friends knew exactly
what to do.

"Get lost, Neal! We're not listening to you!"